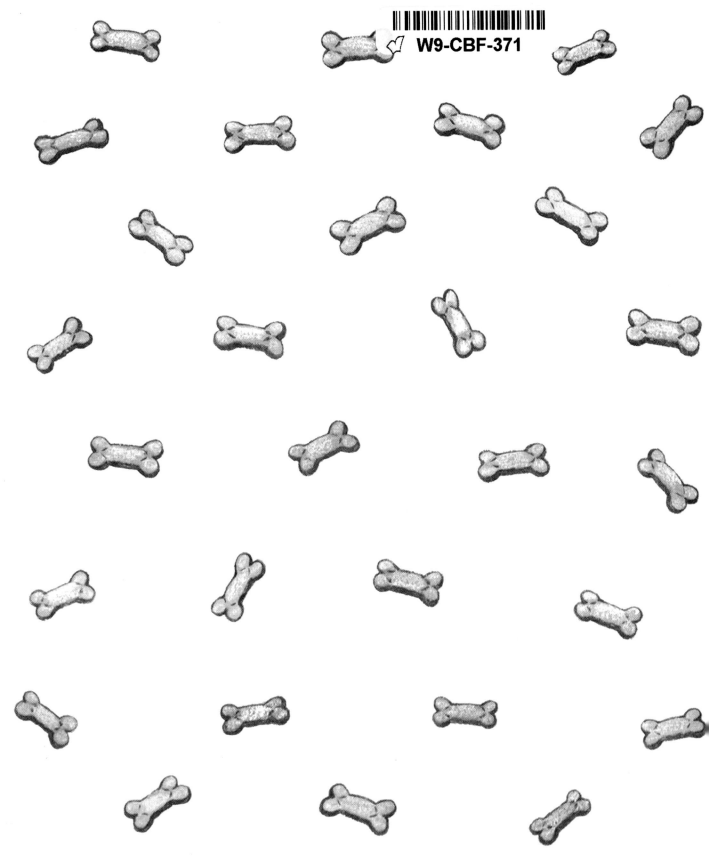

Hello, Biscuit!

story by ALYSSA SATIN CAPUCILLI
pictures by PAT SCHORIES

HarperCollins*Publishers*

"Here we are, puppy," said the little girl.
"Welcome to your new home!"
    Woof, woof!

"The first thing we must do
is find a name for you.
Let's see. You are small and yellow . . ."
        Woof, woof!

"Silly puppy! Come back here!"
Woof!
"You found your bed,
and your bone,
and your biscuits."
Woof, woof!

"But no biscuits yet," said the little girl.
"First we must find a name for you!"

"Let's see. You are small and yellow . . .
Wait, little puppy! Where are you going now?"

Woof, woof!
"You found your ball and your toys."
Woof!
"And you found your biscuits again!"
Woof, woof!

"See?" said the little girl.
"You have everything a puppy could need.
Everything except a name!"
    Woof, woof!

"Now, what is your name going to be?"
    Woof!
"Silly puppy! How did you get those biscuits?"
    Woof, woof!

"Oh no! Come back here with those biscuits!"
Woof, woof, woof, woof!

"That's it!" the little girl cried. "Biscuit!"
  Woof!
"Biscuit is the perfect name for you!"
  Woof, woof!

"Hello, Biscuit!
You found a name all by yourself!"

Woof!

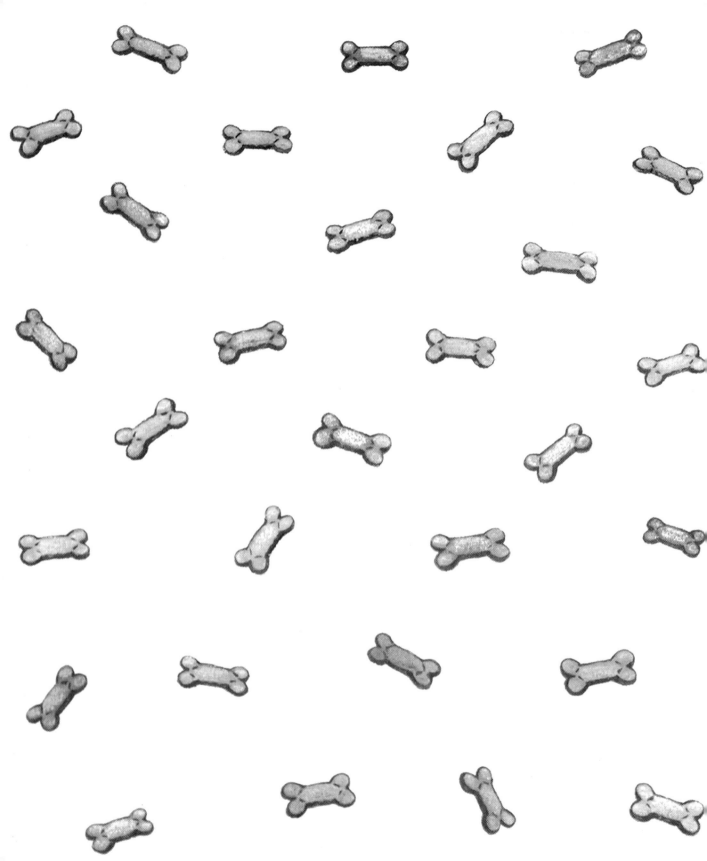